An I Can Read Book®

WHERE IS FREDDY?

Laura Jean Allen

Harper & Row, Publishers

10|90

Library of Congress Cataloging-in-Publication Data
Allen, Laura Jean.
    Where is Freddy?

    (An I can read book)
    Summary: Famous mouse detective Tweedy and his
assistant Rollo investigate the case of wealthy Mrs.
Twombly's missing grandson.
    [1. Mystery and detective stories. 2. Mice—
Fiction] I. Title. II. Series.
PZ7.A4274Wh 1986   [E]   85-45275
ISBN 0-06-020098-7
ISBN 0-06-020099-5 (lib. bdg.)

*To Jeanne and Lisa
with much affection and fond memories
of happy times and feasting
upstairs and down*

Rollo and Tweedy were driving north

on Route 102.

Tweedy was a famous detective.

Rollo was his assistant

and best friend.

At four o'clock sharp

they stopped at the gate

of the Twombly estate.

"What a high wall," said Rollo.

"Ring the bell, Rollo,"

said Detective Tweedy.

"We have a case to solve here."

The great gate opened.

Rollo and Tweedy

drove up to the house.

"Oh, Detective Tweedy,

I am so glad you are here.

My grandson Freddy is missing!"

cried Mrs. Twombly.

"Fear not.

The child will be found,"

said Tweedy.

"When did you last see the boy?"

"At breakfast," said Mrs. Twombly.

"Is there a ransom note?"

asked Rollo.

"No," said Mrs. Twombly.

"What sort of a boy is Freddy?"

asked Tweedy.

"He is a splendid boy,"

said Mrs. Twombly.

"I am sure," said Detective Tweedy,

"but is he active or bookish?"

"Both," said Mrs. Twombly.

"He loves to climb up

on the towers and roof,

and he likes to read

about how to make things."

"Does he have friends?" asked Tweedy.

"His best friend is Tommy,

the gardener's son."

"What kinds of games do they play?"

"All kinds.

They find it great fun

to drop bags of water

from the towers."

"May we look in Freddy's room?"

asked Detective Tweedy.

"Of course," said Mrs. Twombly.

"Look," said Rollo,

"a piece of candy.

Is it a clue?"

"Perhaps," said Tweedy.

"It is saltwater taffy,"

said Mrs. Twombly.

"Freddy won a whole box

for finding someone's balloon."

"Balloon?" asked Tweedy.

"Yes. On the Fourth of July

people around here

send up balloons

with their addresses on them."

"So the balloons can be returned?"

asked Rollo.

"Exactly," said Mrs. Twombly.

"Then whoever sent up the balloon

knows how far it has traveled."

"Is anything missing from the house?"

asked Detective Tweedy.

"Let's ask the servants,"

said Mrs. Twombly.

16

"Forty wire coat hangers are gone,"
said the maid.

"Five of our best sheets
and the laundry basket
are missing," said the housekeeper.

"Somebody has taken

my Swiss chocolate,"

said the cook.

"I was saving it

for my special birthday cake."

"I can't find my driving goggles
and scarf," said the driver.

"My good grass clippers
were in the wet grass,
and I can't find my rope,"
said the gardener.

"How odd," said Rollo.

"Not so odd," said Tweedy.

"I have a hunch

we will find everything—

and Freddy, too."

Rollo and Tweedy searched

until midnight,

but they did not find a single thing.

They got ready for bed.

Suddenly they heard a cry.

Rollo and Tweedy ran

to the window.

"Is that the gardener?"

asked Rollo.

"It is," said Tweedy.

"Is that Freddy with him?"

"It could be," said Tweedy.

"Get the flashlights.

Let's go!"

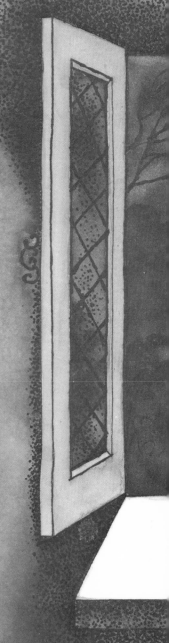

Rollo and Tweedy

crept down the back staircase.

"There!" said Rollo. "Two shadows!"

"Turn off the flashlight,"

said Tweedy.

"We will use the moonlight

to get to the shed.

The gardener probably

took Freddy there."

Rollo and Tweedy tiptoed

into the shed.

"Look!" said Rollo.

Tweedy flashed on his light.

"Shucks!" said Rollo.

"It is only an old coat and hat."

"Let's get some sleep, Rollo.

There is nothing more

we can do tonight," said Tweedy.

"In the morning

we will look for footprints."

The next day

Rollo and Tweedy went out

to look for more clues.

31

"Tweedy!" cried Rollo.

"Freddy is up in that tree!"

Rollo and Tweedy ran to the tree.

"Not quick enough," said Tweedy.

"He is gone."

"But there are footprints
in the mud," said Rollo.

"Indeed," said Tweedy.

"These footprints are the right size
for someone who is two inches tall
and weighs about one ounce."

"Freddy?" asked Rollo.

"Perhaps," said Tweedy.

"Let's follow them."

The footprints led
to the fishpond.

A boy was sitting there.

"Freddy?" asked Rollo.

"No, I am Tommy.

My father is the gardener."

"Were you outside

late last night?" asked Tweedy.

"Yes," said Tommy.

"I was looking

through a telescope,

but I was supposed to be in bed."

"Would you mind if I looked

through the telescope?" asked Tweedy.

"I guess not," said Tommy.

"Very interesting," said Tweedy.

"The case is nearly solved."

"But we have been following

the wrong footprints!" said Rollo.

"They have led us

to an important clue,"

said Detective Tweedy.

"Go ask Mrs. Twombly

to pack a picnic lunch.

Tell the driver

to get the car ready.

I will call the weather station.

Tommy, would you like to come, too?"

"Yes!" said Tommy.

When everything was ready,

they all drove off.

Two hours later

Mrs. Twombly finally asked,

"Where is this wild goose chase
taking us?"

"To your grandson," said Tweedy.

"In a few minutes your Freddy
will appear out of thin air."

"Freddy!" cried Tommy.

40

"Where? Where?" asked Mrs. Twombly.

"Up in the sky," said Rollo.

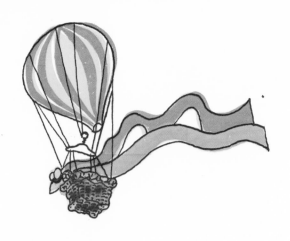

"My Freddy up there

in a balloon?

Impossible!" cried Mrs. Twombly.

"But that *is* Freddy," said Tweedy.

"Freddy made the balloon himself,"

said Tommy.

"He did? How clever,"

said Mrs. Twombly.

"I helped him," said Tommy.

"Freddy got the sheets

and coat hangers

and laundry basket

from the house.

45

I got the rope

and the grass clippers

from the shed.

The goggles and scarf

were my idea, too."

"But Detective Tweedy,
how did you ever guess?"
asked Mrs. Twombly.

"Simple," said Tweedy.

"You yourself told me

about the Fourth of July balloons.

Then I saw a book

about balloon making

in Freddy's room.

The servants told us

what was missing.

When Rollo and I saw Tommy

looking through the telescope,

the case was solved."

49

"I was watching Freddy's balloon,"

said Tommy,

"but I promised not to tell."

"How did he make the balloon fly?"

asked Mrs. Twombly.

"It was all in his book,"

said Tommy.

"But Detective Tweedy,

how did you know

where to look for Freddy?"

asked Mrs. Twombly.

"I called the weather station.

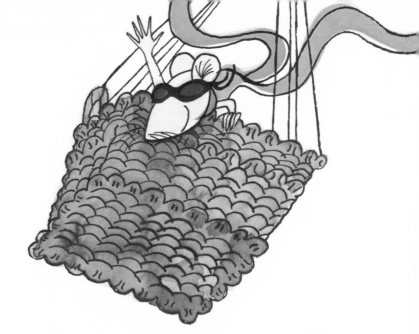

They told me the speed

and direction of the wind.

Freddy has been flying

at that speed and

in that direction.

So I knew we would find him

near Upper Tooting."

"Amazing!" said Mrs. Twombly.

Just then

Freddy's balloon landed.

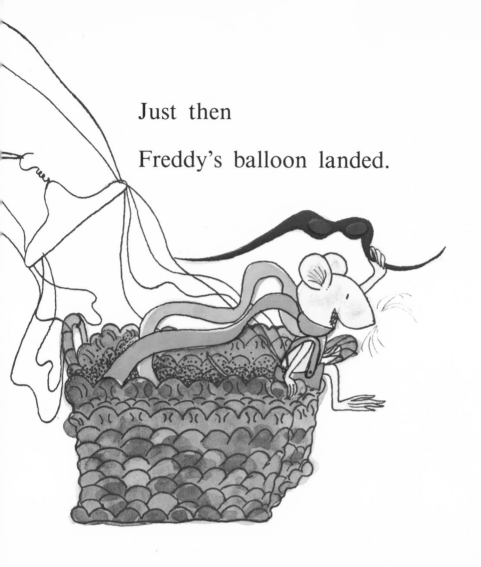

"Freddy!" cried Mrs. Twombly.

"I thought you were kidnapped!"

"I'm sorry, Grandma,"

said Freddy.

"I didn't mean to go

for so long."

53

"I saw you through the telescope,"
said Tommy.

"What was it like?"

"It was fantastic!"

said Freddy.

"You can see the tops of everything,

and the lights at night

are beautiful."

"Well, I am glad

you have landed safely,"

said Mrs. Twombly.

"Can Tommy go with me

the next time?" asked Freddy.

"We will see,"

said Mrs. Twombly.

"But you must not scare Grandma

out of her wits again."

"I promise," said Freddy.

"I'm hungry."

"You are just in time

for a picnic," said Rollo.

Rollo and Tweedy,

Freddy and Tommy,

Mrs. Twombly and the driver,

all ate cheese sandwiches in the grass.

Then they packed up the balloon

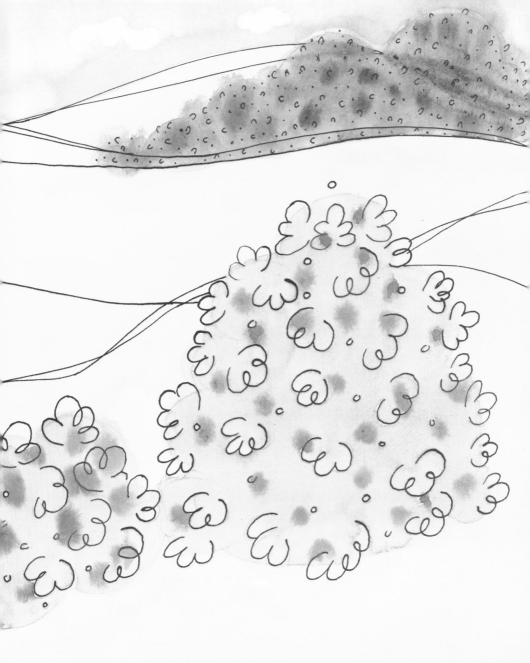

and drove back to the Twombly Estate.

"You are a fine detective

to find my clever grandson,"

said Mrs. Twombly.

"I cannot thank you enough."

"It was no trouble at all,"

said Detective Tweedy.

"Come, Rollo.

We must get back to our office.

There will be new cases to solve."

Rollo and Tweedy

climbed into their little red car

and said good-bye

to Freddy and his grandmother.

Then they sped south

on Route 102.